FAIRY TALE MIX-UPS

Red Riding Hood
Meets
the Three Bears

written by Charlotte Guillain
illustrated by Karl West

HOME

2

One sunny morning, Little Red Riding Hood packed up a basket of cakes and set out to visit her grandma.

"Keep to the path and don't go off into the woods," her mum warned. "The Big Bad Wolf lives there."

"I will," said Little Red Riding Hood.

But the path was **overgrown** and soon Little Red Riding Hood was lost! She didn't notice Goldilocks walking in the other direction.

The Big Bad Wolf was happy. "Two little girls lost in the woods," he muttered with a **sly** grin. "More *food for me.*"

Then he set off after Goldilocks.

Little Red Riding Hood finally arrived at a small cottage.

"Oh!" she **gasped**. "That's strange. I thought Grandma lived in a blue house. Maybe she painted it."

The door was open. Little Red Riding Hood went inside.

"Grandma!" she called. "Where are you?"

"Three bowls of porridge!" said Little Red Riding Hood. "What a big breakfast you have, Grandma!"

Little Red Riding Hood tidied the bowls of porridge away. Then she got out her cakes and put them on a plate.

"Grandma!" she called. "Where are you?"

Little Red Riding Hood went to look in the living room.

"What big chairs you have, Grandma!" she said.

It was strange. Grandma had painted the house and bought three new chairs.

Little Red Riding Hood looked all around for her grandma.

"Grandma!" she called. "Where are you?"

Then Little Red Riding Hood went upstairs to see if Grandma was having a nap.

She opened the door and peered inside the bedroom. She saw three new beds!

"My, what a loud snore you have, Grandma!" said Little Red Riding Hood.

She turned on the light and shouted, "Wake up!"

The three bears woke up.

Little Red Riding Hood screamed and ran downstairs. The three bears ran after her.

"Don't be scared!" called Mother Bear.

"Cakes!" said Baby Bear when he saw the plate on the table.

"They are for my grandma," said Little Red Riding Hood.

"You've come to the wrong house," said Father Bear.

The three bears took Little Red Riding Hood through the woods to her grandma's house.

But when they arrived, Little Red Riding Hood **gasped**, "Oh no!"

The Big Bad Wolf was about to eat Grandma and Goldilocks!

Just then, the three bears gave a great big ...

... ROAR!

The Big Bad Wolf screamed and ran away.

"Well," said Grandma, "that was a strange day."

"At least we still have the cakes," said Little Red Riding Hood.

"Then let's finish the day with a tea party," said Grandma.

And that's what they did.

Little Red Riding Hood

Little Red Riding Hood was first written down by the Brothers Grimm. They lived in Germany 200 years ago. They called the story *Little Red-Cap*. Little Red-Cap is sent to visit her grandmother and meets a wolf on the way. The wolf goes ahead to Grandmother's house and eats her! The wolf then puts on Grandmother's clothes and waits for Little Red-Cap. When she arrives, the wolf eats her, too! Luckily a hunter cuts Little Red-Cap and Grandmother out of the wolf's stomach.

Goldilocks and the Three Bears

Goldilocks is a traditional British story. When it was first written down, it was called *The Story of the Three Bears*. It is about an old woman who goes into the three bears' house. She eats the baby bear's porridge, breaks his chair and sleeps in his bed. When the bears come back and wake her up, she runs away.

Glossary

gasp – breathe in quickly in surprise

overgrown – covered with plants and weeds

sly – secretive and cunning

Writing prompts

If you could be a character in this story, who would you choose? Why?

Imagine you are Baby Bear. Write a letter to Little Red Riding Hood to say thank you for the tea party.

Write some instructions for other children going through the woods to visit Grandma. How can they stay safe?

Read more

Goldilocks and the Three Bears, Kate Daubney
(Tiger Tales, 2015)

Goldilocks and the Three Bears, Vera Southgate
(Ladybird, 2012)

Little Red and the Very Hungry Lion, Alex T. Smith
(Scholastic, 2015)

Little Red Riding Hood, Loretta Schauer (Tiger Tales, 2015)

Websites

www.bbc.co.uk/cbeebies/stories/melody-red-riding-hood
This video uses music in a retelling of *Little Red Riding Hood*.

www.bbc.co.uk/wales/snapdragon/yesflash/story.htm
Read the original story of *Goldilocks and the Three Bears* on
this website.

www.readwritethink.org/files/resources/interactives/fairy-tales
Visit this website to write your own mixed-up fairy tale!

Read all the books in the series:

FAIRY TALE MIX-UPS
The Frog Prince Saves Sleeping Beauty
written by Charlotte Guillain · Illustrated by Dan Widdowson

FAIRY TALE MIX-UPS
The Elves Help Puss In Boots
written by Paul Harrison · Illustrated by Tim Sutcliffe

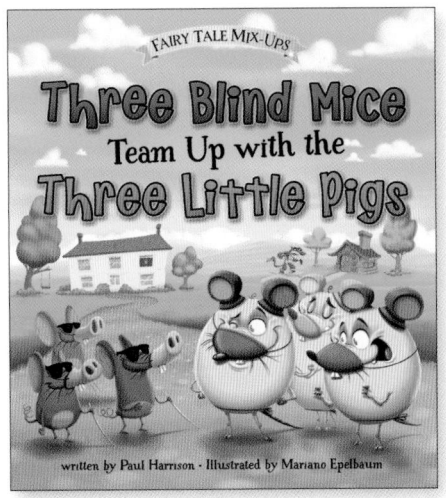

FAIRY TALE MIX-UPS
Three Blind Mice Team Up with the Three Little Pigs
written by Paul Harrison · Illustrated by Mariano Epelbaum

FAIRY TALE MIX-UPS
Red Riding Hood Meets the Three Bears
written by Charlotte Guillain · Illustrated by Karl West

Visit www.raintree.co.uk

Raintree is an imprint of Capstone Global Library Limited, a company incorporated in England and Wales having its registered office at 264 Banbury Road, Oxford, OX2 7DY – Registered company number: 6695582

www.raintree.co.uk
myorders@raintree.co.uk

Edited by Penny West
Designed by Steve Mead
Original illustrations © Capstone Global Library Ltd 2016
Illustrated by Karl West, Astound US
Production by Steve Walker
Originated by Capstone Global Library Limited
Printed and bound in China

ISBN 978 1 474 72756 3
20 19 18 17 16
10 9 8 7 6 5 4 3 2 1

British Library Cataloguing in Publication Data
A full catalogue record for this book is available from the British Library.